PIRATE

The Story of a Buccaneer

Dee Phillips

READZONE

READZONE

First published in this edition 2014

The right of the Author to be identified as the Author of this work has been asserted by the Author in accordance with the Copyright, Designs and Patents Act 1988

Every attempt has been made by the Publisher to secure appropriate permissions for material reproduced in this book. If there has been any oversight we will be happy to rectify the situation in future editions or reprints. Written submissions should be made to the Publishers.

British Library Cataloguing in Publication Data (CIP) is available for this title.

ISBN 978-1-78322-514-9

Printed in Malta by Melita Press

Developed and Created by Ruby Tuesday Books Ltd
Project Director – Ruth Owen
Designers – Emma Randall and Elaine Wilkinson

Images courtesy of Shutterstock.

Acknowledgements
With thanks to Lorraine Petersen, Educational Consultant, for her help in the development and creation of these books

Visit our website: www.readzonebooks.com

I have gold and silver.

I have precious jewels.

I am rich beyond my wildest dreams.

But my dreams have become a nightmare.

PIRATE
The Story of a Buccaneer

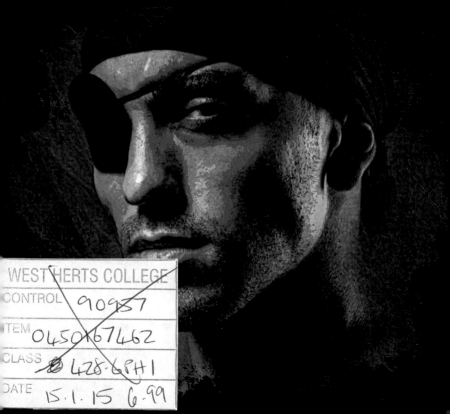

In the 1600s and 1700s, merchant ships carried cargo around the world.

They carried silks, cotton, iron, gunpowder, brandy and wine.

Some carried treasure from South America. Gold and silver and precious jewels.

The merchant ships were not alone on the ocean.

Violent, ruthless criminals sailed the seas in search of treasure.

The merchant ships could be attacked at any time.

Attacked by...

PIRATES

I cough up rum and water.
Blood trickles from my face.
I force open the chest with
my knife.

Gold and silver.

Precious jewels.

I laugh like a crazy man.

I laugh like a crazy man.
I am rich beyond my
wildest dreams.

But I'm no rich gentleman.
Some would say I'm evil.
A thief. A pirate.

So how did I come to sail
on a pirate ship?

I was born in the docks.

I never knew my father.
My mother died of a fever.

I soon became a thief.
A little thief with an empty belly.
I picked the pockets of gentlemen.
I dreamed of being rich.

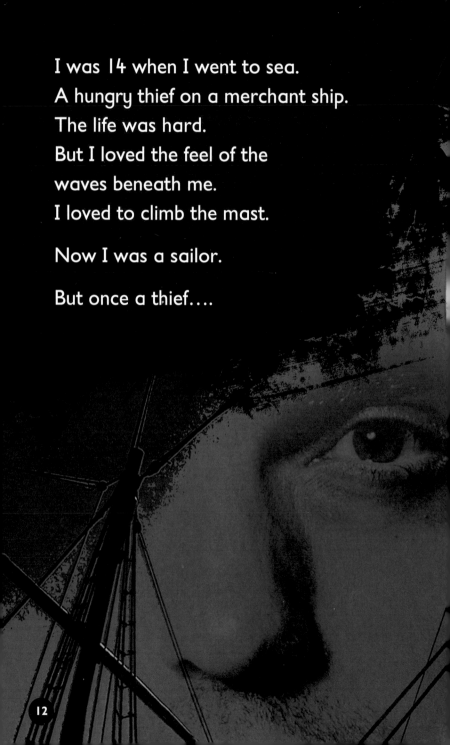

I was 14 when I went to sea.
A hungry thief on a merchant ship.
The life was hard.
But I loved the feel of the
waves beneath me.
I loved to climb the mast.

Now I was a sailor.

But once a thief....

One night, I served the
captain his supper.
I thought he had fallen asleep.
I drank his wine.
I ate his food.

But the captain was not asleep.
"You evil little thief!" he hissed.

His whip tore at my face
and chest.

One day, I was on watch.
A ship appeared.
Then up went a black flag.

PIRATES!

We fired our guns.
We tried to escape, but we
were too slow.
The pirates attacked
like demons.
Demons with pistols, axes
and cutlasses.

The pirates tied up our captain.
They put burning matches
in his eyes.
"Where's the gold?"
a pirate hissed.
But we carried no gold.

The pirates took silks,
brandy and gunpowder.
They stole all our food and
fresh water.

"Will you join us?" a pirate asked.
My belly was empty.
My face and chest had
scars from my captain's whip.

I helped the pirates toss my
captain overboard.

I cough up rum and water.
Blood trickles from my face.

Now I have gold and silver.
Now I am rich beyond my
wildest dreams.

So what was it like to
sail on a pirate ship?

Now I was a pirate.
I sailed on a ship with
men of all colours.
I loved the feel of the
waves beneath me.
I loved to climb the mast.

We set sail for warm oceans.
We lay on the deck in the
burning sun.
Our bellies full of roasted turtle.
Our bodies weak with wine and rum.

One day, a storm blew up.
Waves as high as mountains
lashed the ship.
I clung to the deck as water
washed over me.

One man's leg was
crushed by a barrel.
We filled him with rum.
Then we held him down.
The ship's carpenter
fetched his tools....

We attacked many ships.
We took silks, cotton
and brandy.
We stole ropes, gunpowder,
food and fresh water.
Sometimes we found
coins or jewels.

I was paid my fair share.
But when we went ashore,
it was soon spent.

I cough up rum and water.
Blood trickles from my face.
I look at the riches in
the chest.
And laugh like a crazy man.

So how did this pirate
become rich beyond his
wildest dreams?

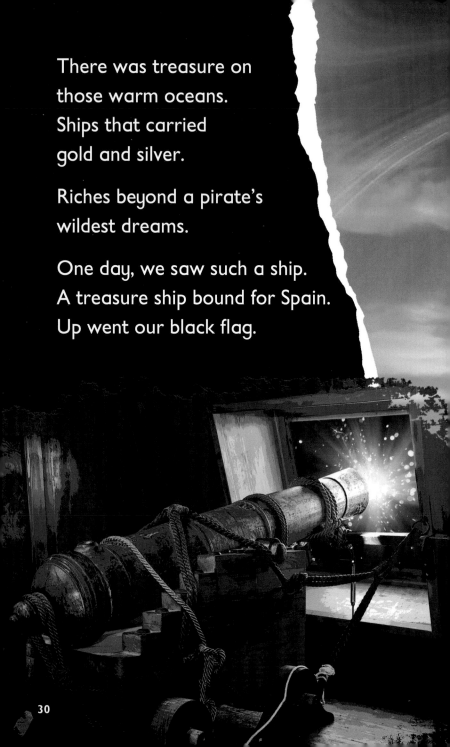

There was treasure on
those warm oceans.
Ships that carried
gold and silver.

Riches beyond a pirate's
wildest dreams.

One day, we saw such a ship.
A treasure ship bound for Spain.
Up went our black flag.

They fired their guns.
We fired back.
They tried to escape, but we
were too fast.

We swarmed onto their ship.
We murdered some men.
We tied up others.
The ship was loaded with
gold and silver.
Emeralds, rubies and
other precious jewels.

Riches beyond my wildest dreams.

When we sailed away, our ship
was heavy.
Heavy with stolen treasure.

That night we were crazy with
wine and rum.
We sang and fired our guns.
We toasted the devil and the
Spanish king.

We didn't see the storm.

The storm that
came closer
and closer.

Waves as high as mountains
lashed the ship.
Her timbers creaked
and cracked.
Our treasure was
washed overboard.

The mast snapped, crashing
into the sea.
I clung to the deck as the
ship broke apart.

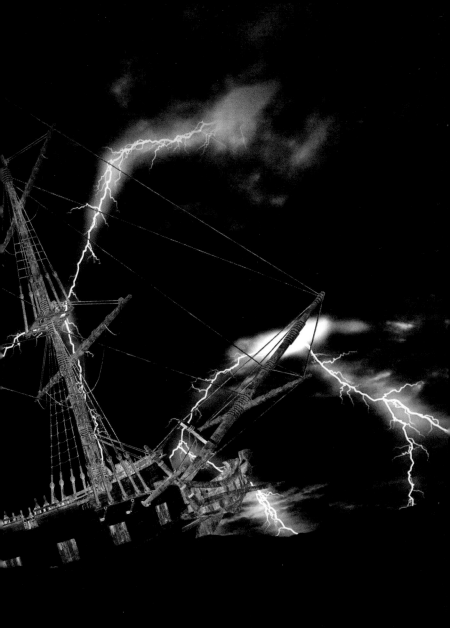

When I came to, the storm had passed.
A chest lay beside me.
A chest and a bottle of rum.
That was when I knew I was rich.

Rich beyond my wildest dreams.
But my dreams have become a nightmare.

I look around me.
I see rocks and ocean.
No beast. No plant. No fresh water.
I laugh like a crazy man.

A crazy man washed up in hell.

I know one day a ship will come.

They'll find gold and silver and
precious jewels.

And the sun-baked bones of
a pirate.

A pirate rich beyond his
wildest dreams....

PIRATE:
Behind the Story

For as long as cargo, or merchant, ships have sailed the world's oceans, there have been pirates ready to steal the goods they carry.

Pirates in the 1600s and 1700s (the period when the story is set) were also known as buccaneers. Many began their careers as sailors on merchant ships or in the navy. Life in these centuries was hard, however, at sea and on land. Many sailors turned to a life of crime on a pirate ship as a way to make their fortune and escape hardship.

A pirate ship might have a crew of 80 to 100 members. The pirates in one crew often came from many different countries and cultures. A pirate crew voted for their captain. Important decisions, such as where to sail to, were also decided by a vote. Every pirate crew had a written agreement, called a set of articles. This agreement listed the rules for life on board ship. It also detailed how any loot would be divided up between the crew.

If a pirate ship was captured by the navy, the pirates might be sentenced to death by hanging.

Treasure Ships

From the 1500s until the 1700s, Spanish ships carried gold, silver and precious jewels from South America back to Spain. Before it was sent to Spain, silver and gold was made into coins. Silver coins were known as pieces of eight. Gold coins were called doubloons. The cargo of one of these Spanish "treasure ships" would be worth millions of pounds in today's money.

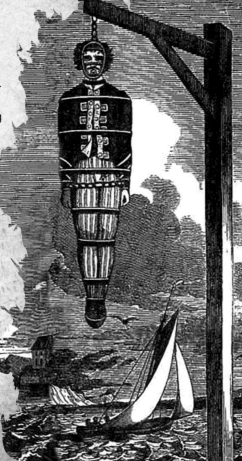

After hanging, a pirate's dead body might be placed in a gibbet and hung up in the docks as a warning to other pirates. This was known as "hanging in chains".

PIRATE - What's next?

MESSAGE IN A BOTTLE
ON YOUR OWN

At the end of the story, the pirate is trapped on a tiny island. He knows he will not survive to enjoy his riches. Imagine you are the doomed pirate. Write a final letter to be thrown out to sea in the empty rum bottle. What do you want to tell the world about your life as a pirate? Are you sorry for living a life of crime? What are your final days and hours like marooned on the island?

PIRATE 2
ON YOUR OWN / WITH A PARTNER / IN A GROUP

Many movies have an ending that allows for a sequel.
Think up a plot for *PIRATE 2*, the sequel to the pirate's story.

- How does the pirate get off the island?

- What does he do next? Does he go on to become a rich man, or does he lose his treasure chest to an enemy?

Real-life pirates often wore similar clothes to sailors on merchant and navy ships. Then they customised their outfits with objects they stole such as expensive velvet jackets and elaborate hats and jewellery. Some pirates had many scars and missing body parts such as a leg, hand or eye.

Imagine you are a costume designer creating the look for an 18th century pirate in a new movie. Draw or use a computer to create your pirate character's costume. Will your pirate look stylish, flamboyant and sexy? Or will he be filthy, ugly and terrifying?

Thanks to the glamorous pirate characters in many books and movies, historical pirates are often thought of as exciting and romantic. In reality, however, pirates were criminals who sometimes tortured and murdered their victims.

• How did you feel about the pirate character in the book? Did you sympathise with his decision to become a pirate? Did you like or dislike the character?

• At the end of the story, did you feel sorry for the pirate, or did you feel he deserved his terrible fate?

Titles in the

Yesterday's Voices

series

We jump from our ship and attack. But something feels wrong. I know this place....

We face each other. Two proud samurai. Revenge burns in my heart.

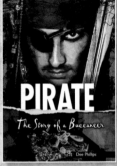

We saw a treasure ship. Up went our black flag. They could not escape....

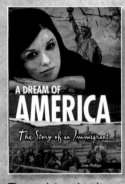

The work is so hard. I miss my home. Will my dream of America come true?

I jumped from the plane. I carried fake papers, a gun and a radio. Now I was Sylvie, a resistance fighter....

Every day we went on patrol. The Viet Cong hid in jungles and villages. We had to find them, before they found us.

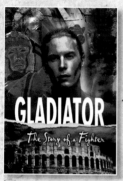

GLADIATOR
The Story of a Fighter

I waited deep below the arena. Then it was my turn to fight. Kill or be killed!

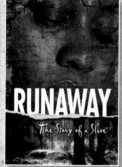

RUNAWAY
The Story of a Slave

I cannot live as a slave any longer. Tonight, I will escape and never go back.

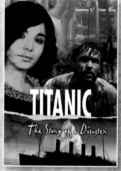

TITANIC
The Story of a Disaster

The ship is sinking into the icy sea. I don't want to die. Someone help us!

OVER THE TOP
The Story of a Soldier

I'm waiting in the trench. I am so afraid. Tomorrow we go over the top.

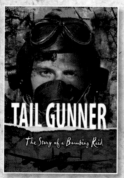

TAIL GUNNER
The Story of a Bombing Raid

Another night. Another bombing raid. Will this night be the one when we don't make it back?

HOLOCAUST
The Story of a Survivor

They took my clothes and shaved my head. I was no longer a human.